For my mother, Dorcas. You gave me life and showed me how to live it with purpose. For my wife, Julia. Life is everything because you're in it! For my sister, Hopenet, Granny Hope, Mahm Sandy, and Aunty Pam. Thanks for always believing in me. For my daughter Cienna and Black girls everywhere, you are full of magic and awesome power! The world is yours!

—AK

To my mother, Wanda, whose strength to fight for life and sincere desire to educate showed me the courage to lead and read by example; and to my daughters Opal and Stella and all Black and brown girls around the world to always dream BIG!

—JR

For my mama, who deserves the world.

—AQ

Text © 2024 by Ali Kamanda and Jorge Redmond
Illustrations © 2024 by Amanda Quartey
Cover and internal design © 2024 by Sourcebooks
Sourcebooks and the colophon are registered trademarks of Sourcebooks.
All artwork was created in Procreate on the iPad Pro 4th Gen.
Published by Sourcebooks eXplore, an imprint of Sourcebooks Kids
P.O. Box 4410, Naperville, Illinois 60567-4410
(630) 961-3900
sourcebookskids.com
Cataloging-in-Publication Data is on file with the Library of Congress.
Source of Production: Worzalla, Stevens Point, Wisconsin, USA
Date of Production: September 2024
Run Number: 5044959
Printed and bound in the United States of America.
WOZ 10 9 8 7 6 5 4 3 2 1

BLACK GIRL, BLACK GIRL

CELEBRATE THE POWER OF YOU

WRITTEN BY
ALI KAMANDA AND
JORGE REDMOND

PICTURES BY
AMANDA QUARTEY

sourcebooks
eXplore

Dear girl, Black girl,
rise up, it's time.
It's a new day and a
chance to shine.

Shine like the moon,
you're one of a kind.
Radiant and fierce, a
brilliant young mind.

A mind filled with wonder, creativity and dreams. Shape your own history like these amazing queens.

Dear girl,
 Black girl,
  what do you see?

That's Kamala Harris,
America's 49th VP.

This is just the beginning,
so much more to behold.

There's Wilma Rudolph,
three Olympic medals,
all gold.

Take a breath,
  close your eyes,
    and now picture this feat:

A young Claudette Colvin
wouldn't give up her bus seat.

Dear girl,
    Black girl,
        what's that music you hear?

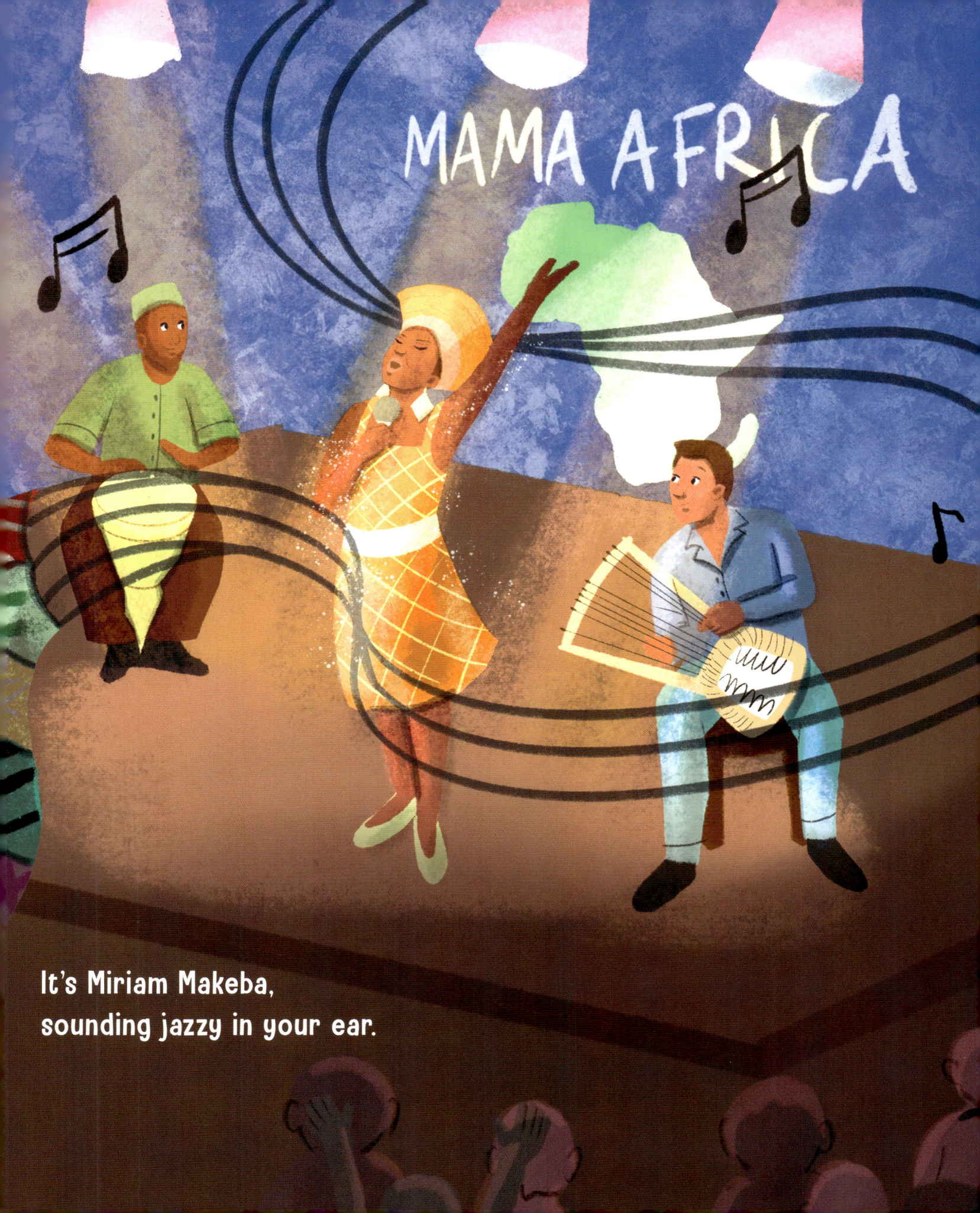

MAMA AFRICA

It's Miriam Makeba,
sounding jazzy in your ear.

Now I wonder,
dear girl,
if you've ever been taught

of Mae Carol Jemison, first Black female astronaut.

Learn your rich history,
    it's your roots, your foundation.

That's why Adelaide Casely-Hayford championed education.

Dear girl,
  Black girl,
    ever dream you could fly?

Watch Misty Copeland gracefully jeté to the sky.

Live life,
you trailblazer,
with courage and focus.

Viola Desmond was a businesswoman with purpose.

In the end, my dear girl,
   write your story your way.

You can be a creative visionary, like Ava DuVernay.

Dear girl, Black girl, what do you see?
I see so many faces that look like me.

Indeed, precious girl, all these faces you see were once like you, uncertain of their destiny.

Rise with passion, your journey starts today. An adventure awaits, there's no time for delay.

Dear girl, Black girl, this one is written for you.
There's no one on Earth who can do what you do.

Born to be great, your excellence shines from within.
You own half the sky, but your poetry's yet written.

Go change the world, make it a better place.
Trust in your fierce spirit and magnificent grace.

Dear girl, Black girl,
I believe in you so.

Let's start your journey—
ready,
set,
go.

A quilt is a multi-layered textile, traditionally comprising two or more layers of fabric. There is a sense of pride and self-esteem connected with quilting. Quilts provide a record of their cultural and political past. During the Civil Rights Movement, the Freedom Quilting Bee was established as a way for African American women to gain economic independence. The quilts of Gee's Bend are some of the most important African American visual and cultural contributions to the history of American art.

KAMALA HARRIS (born October 20, 1964) is a politician and an attorney who became the 49th vice president of the United States. She is not only the first female vice president, but she is also the first African American and first Asian American U.S. vice president. Before her tenure in the White House, she had previously served as the attorney general of California and as a senator representing California in the U.S. Congress.

WILMA RUDOLPH

(June 23, 1940–November 12, 1994) became the first American woman to win three gold medals for track and field in a single Olympic Games. In the 1960s, she was considered the fastest woman in the world. She is also known for being a civil rights and women's rights activist.

CLAUDETTE COLVIN (born September 5, 1939) was a pioneer activist in the Civil Rights Movement. She is best known for being arrested at the age of fifteen for refusing to give up her seat on a segregated bus. This happened nine months before Rosa Parks's protest. Colvin's protest helped lead to the Montgomery bus boycott in 1955. A year later in 1956, in the case Browder v. Gayle, Colvin was one of four other women who went to the Supreme Court to successfully challenge the law regarding public bus segregation. The Supreme Court ruled it unconstitutional and ordered Alabama and Montgomery to desegregate their buses. In 2018, Colvin received a Congressional honor for her lifetime commitment to public service.

MIRIAM MAKEBA

(March 4, 1932–November 9, 2008) was a South African singer, songwriter, actress, United Nations goodwill ambassador, and civil rights activist. Nicknamed Mama Africa, she was one of the first artists to bring African music into the Western mainstream. Makeba was also an advocate against apartheid in South Africa and included some of those messages in her music. She received a Grammy Award for her 1965 album, *An Evening with Belafonte/Makeba*.

MAE CAROL JEMISON (born October 17, 1956) is the first Black woman to go to space. Jemison graduated high school at age sixteen and joined NASA after studying chemical engineering and African American Studies in college. She orbited the Earth aboard the space shuttle *Endeavour* for nearly eight days. She has been inducted into the National Women's Hall of Fame and the International Space Hall of Fame.

ADELAIDE CASELY-HAYFORD (June 2, 1868–January 24, 1960) was a Sierra Leone Creole educational advocate, activist of cultural nationalism, short story writer, and feminist. She paved the way for young girls in her home country to be able to go to school and learn skills that they otherwise might not have been able to learn on their own. She was awarded the King's Silver Jubilee Medal, and in 1978, asteroid 6848 Casely-Hayford was named in her memory.

MISTY COPELAND (born September 10, 1982) is a ballet dancer for American Ballet Theatre (ABT), one of the top classical ballet companies in the United States. On June 30, 2015, Copeland became the first African American woman to be promoted to principal dancer at ABT. Also in 2015, she was named one of the 100 most influential people in the world by *Time* magazine and appeared on its cover.

VIOLA DESMOND (July 6, 1914–February 7, 1965) was a Canadian civil rights activist and businesswoman. She went on to become a successful entrepreneur, operating a beauty school as well as her own salon. She became the first Canadian woman to appear alone on a Canadian bank note, a $10 bill. She also helped start the modern civil rights movement in Canada by challenging racial segregation by refusing to leave a whites-only area of a movie theater.

AVA DUVERNAY (born August 24, 1972) is a director, producer, and screenwriter. She became the first Black woman to win the U.S. Directing Award: Dramatic category at the 2012 Sundance Film Festival. For her work on *Selma*, she became the first Black woman to be nominated for a Golden Globe Award for Best Director, and the first Black female director to have her film nominated for the Academy Award for Best Picture.